The Boy W

retold by Pam Holden
illustrated by Samer Hatam

Hundreds of years ago, a young boy was given an important job to do while his parents worked. He was told to spend the days on a rocky hilltop near his village, guarding the family's flock of sheep. There were several dangers for the sheep if they wandered away from the flock: in winter they could get lost in deep snow or fall over a cliff in thick fog; occasionally a daring thief would try to steal one for its valuable wool and meat; sometimes a hungry wolf would come out of the nearby woods to hunt one for a feast.

At sunset every day, the sheep were driven downhill into a wooden shed, where they were sheltered from the weather and safe from any danger. Then the boy spent the evenings playing with his friends and relaxing at his home in the village.

All through the long summer months, he watched the sheep calmly grazing without any trouble, but he found the job extremely boring. "Every day is exactly the same!" he grumbled to himself. "I wish something exciting would happen. I need an adventure – I almost wish a thief or a wolf would come!" As he sat on the hilltop hour after hour, the boy dreamed of being a hero who did something brave. But every day passed slowly without any challenges, until he finally decided to create some excitement for himself.

He stood facing the direction of the village, cupped his hands around his mouth, and shouted in his loudest voice, "Wolf! Wolf! Help!" His cries were heard by the adults busy at their work.

Immediately the men grabbed weapons and raced up the hillside to rescue the boy and his flock, but when they arrived there was no wolf in sight.

After a thorough search was made, everyone agreed that the wolf had disappeared, so the danger had passed. Before returning to their work, they told the boy to shout loudly for help if he saw any further sign of the wolf.

When he was alone again, the boy laughed about what had happened. "That was so funny to watch!" he chuckled to himself. "All those silly people searching busily for something that wasn't even there!" He felt pleased that he had caused some excitement, with worried people rushing up the hill to hunt an imaginary wolf!

Only one week later, the boy became bored again and remembered how he had enjoyed fooling those villagers who tried to help him. He repeated the trick, shouting downhill toward the village, "Help! Wolf! The wolf is back!" As he expected, there was a frantic rush of rescuers dashing up the hill, hoping to save the sheep.

14

Just as the previous time, the boy was secretly amused to see the villager's weapons and watch their unsuccessful efforts to find the non-existent wolf. When he tried to hide a sly smile, some people noticed and became suspicious, questioning him angrily. His answer was to confess with a grin, "I fooled you just like last week! There was never any wolf at all – it was only a joke!"

All the men were astonished that the boy had dared to call them away from their important work for such a silly trick. "You are wicked to waste our valuable time," said one man.

"Don't expect us to ever help you again," grumbled another.

"You needn't bother repeating that nasty trick," a third man shouted as they left the hillside. "We are much too busy to answer your smart calls." The boy didn't say he was sorry because he still thought it was harmless fun.

However, a few weeks later, the boy could hardly believe his eyes when he spotted a large wolf creeping out of the woods, stalking the fattest sheep. As it came toward the flock, the boy screamed to the villagers, "Wolf! Wolf! Help!" His loud, desperate cries were heard clearly by the men, but they immediately thought that this was another of the boy's senseless jokes, so they continued working.

"How can he try that false alarm again?" the villagers asked each other in amazement. "He can't expect us to believe him for a third time!" While the usual work continued in the village, the wolf caught the sheep he was stalking. There was nothing the boy could do, except to save the rest of the flock by rounding them up and driving them downhill to the safety of the night shelter.

When the villagers heard what had happened, they told the foolish boy that the sad loss of his valuable sheep was his own fault. They hoped he had learned a lesson: people who lie and play tricks will not be believed even when they do tell the truth. For hundreds of years, everyone who ever heard this story has remembered that it is unwise to ask for help unless it is really needed. There is a well-known saying: ***"Don't cry wolf!"***